ABOU.

AMBUSH IN THE AMAZON
Walter Dean Myers

Camping in the lush rain forest along the Amazon River seemed like an ideal vacation for Chris and Ken Arrow— until the appearance of a gigantic creature from the swamp. The Quechuan tribe is sure the *monstruo*, a legendary creature that once terrorized their people, has returned. But the Arrows think something's not right about the monster's sudden reappearance. And when their camp is ravaged by unknown saboteurs, they know it has to be more than coincidence. But finding out who is responsible for the attacks won't be easy, as they must simultaneously combat the superstitions of the tribesmen and the perils of the Amazon jungle. And more dangers lie ahead, as the Quechuan people plan the one thing said to stop the creature: a human sacrifice.

Chris and Ken's travels with their mother, famous anthropologist Carla Arrow, take them to a land of great tropical beauty and fast-paced adventure in this action-packed story.

AMBUSH
IN THE AMAZON

ALSO BY WALTER DEAN MYERS

Adventure in Granada
The Black Pearl & the Ghost
Duel in the Desert
Fast Sam, Cool Clyde, and Stuff
The Golden Serpent
The Hidden Shrine
The Legend of Tarik
Mojo and the Russians
Motown and Didi
The Nicholas Factor
Won't Know Till I Get There
The Young Landlords

AMBUSH IN THE AMAZON

BY

WALTER DEAN MYERS

PUFFIN BOOKS

PUFFIN BOOKS
Viking Penguin Inc., 40 West 23rd Street, New York, New York 10010, U.S.A.
Penguin Books Ltd, Harmondsworth, Middlesex, England
Penguin Books Australia Ltd, Ringwood, Victoria, Australia
Penguin Books Canada Limited, 2801 John Street,
Markham, Ontario, Canada L3R 1B4
Penguin Books (N.Z.) Ltd, 182–190 Wairau Road, Auckland 10, New Zealand

First published in Puffin Books 1986
Published simultaneously in Canada
Copyright © Walter Dean Myers, 1986
All rights reserved
Printed in U.S.A. by R. R. Donnelley & Sons Company, Harrisonburg, Virginia
Set in Trump

Library of Congress Cataloging in Publication Data
Myers, Walter Dean.   Ambush in the Amazon.
Summary: While camping in the Amazon, Chris and his brother, Ken, try to
save a tribal village from the attacks of what appears to be a reincarnated
swamp monster.
[1. Adventure and adventurers—Fiction.   2. Amazon River Valley—Fiction]
I. Title.
PZ7.M992Am   1986   [Fic]   85-43409   ISBN 0-14-032102-0

CONTENTS

AMBUSH
IN THE AMAZON

CHAPTER 1

"Did you hear anything?" Ken asked.

"Not a thing. Go to sleep," I answered. I was exhausted. We had been in Peru three days and busy every moment of them.

"Chris, I think I heard something," my brother whispered in the darkness.

"Ken, we're in the middle of the Amazon jungle," I said, my eyes still closed. "There are all kinds of birds and small animals making noises outside. There aren't any large animals so we don't have to be nervous."

"Yeah, okay," Ken said.

"Now go to sleep, please!"

The sounds of the jungle *were* kind of weird but I didn't want to babysit for Ken all night. The two cots in the tent were covered with netting to keep us from being eaten up by mosquitoes.

"Chris?"

"Go to sleep!"

I let a few minutes pass.

"Ken?"

I listened carefully. In between the screeching of the birds and occasional yelps of small animals I could hear Ken's steady breathing. He was finally asleep.

I had just started to doze off myself when I felt the wind stir the mosquito netting. I pulled the sheet up around my neck and turned slightly. Then I smelled something really foul. I couldn't figure out what it was, but I figured that it would go away as soon as the wind shifted.

I was ready for a good night's sleep. The morning would be soon enough to think about Mom's project.

Graaarrrr!

There was a low sound, more like a growl than a human voice, and it sounded as if it was right in the tent! I took a deep breath and hoped that I was hearing things. Maybe I was only tired.

Graaarrrr!

I felt a cold chill up my spine and I knew it wasn't the wind.

"Ken? That you fooling around?"

GRAAARRRGH! GRAAARRGH!

I felt something ripping at the netting! Then the cot was shaking!

GRAAARRGH! GRAAARRGH!

As I tried to sit up, something hit me on the side of the

4

head. I wanted to move away but I was tangled in the covers. I tried to kick out at it the best I could but all I could feel was the mosquito netting.

GRAAARRRGH!

"Ken!" I called to my brother. "Wake up!"

Just then I felt a burning sensation on my shoulder. Something came toward my face and I grabbed it. It felt like a huge hairy paw! I could feel the claws as it pushed toward my eyes and I screamed.

"Ken! Ken! Please! Wake up!"

I held the thing away from my face but it seemed all over me. The smell was terrible. It was after my shoulder again. It felt as if it was trying to bite me. It was huge!

"Ken, plea . . ." It smothered me with its hairy body. I couldn't breathe. I felt myself being half pushed, half lifted out of the cot. I twisted as best I could and landed hard on the ground.

I couldn't tell what was going on. I tried to fight free of the netting and hit my wrist hard against something. Then I lay still.

For what seemed a long time I didn't move. I didn't hear anything, either, except the sound of my own breathing. I was afraid of moving and afraid of not moving.

Slowly I untangled myself. The terrible smell was still there but I didn't hear any noise. I thought about Ken.

I got to my feet as quietly as I could. The inside of the tent was pitch-black. I knew there was a flashlight on the table between the two cots and I reached for it. My hand was trembling as I picked it up. I fumbled for the switch and turned it on.

My cot was a shambles. The netting was torn down. I looked over at Ken's cot. He wasn't moving. I went over and shook his shoulder.

"Ken?" I said softly.

He stirred, and turned away from me, still asleep. For a moment I didn't know what to do. I sat down on Ken's cot and looked at the torn netting. I wondered if I had been dreaming, but the smell still filled our tent.

"Ken?" I said louder. Maybe I was seventeen and he was only fourteen, but I needed someone to talk to. "Ken!"

He sat up sleepily and pushed himself up on one elbow. "What's up?" he said, drowsily.

"I just had one heck of a bad dream," I said.

"Oh, yeah?" He looked over at me. "What did you dream about?"

"Being attacked by monsters," I said. It already seemed a little silly.

"What happened to your shoulder?" he asked.

I looked at my shoulder. There were three long scratches, like the kind an animal's paw would make, that ran from the top of my shoulder halfway down my arm. They were bleeding lightly.

"I might have . . ." I was going to tell him that I might have scratched myself when I was dreaming, but now I wasn't sure.

"What kind of dream was it?" he asked, sitting up.

"I thought it was a dream," I said. "I dreamed that something was jumping at me, and that I felt claws."

"Something that would leave a print like that on the sheet?" he asked.

I looked at the sheet and saw a print that was as long as a bear's, but much more narrow. There were two holes in the sheet where the claws would have been.

"Look, what do you think we should do?" I said.

"You want to just tremble a little and be scared?" Ken asked.

"We'll just stay put," I said. "Tarija will be back in the morning. She'll know what to do."

"If we're still alive in the morning," Ken said.

"It was probably some small animal," I said.

"With big feet," Ken added.

"We probably scared it as much as it scared us."

"Maybe we can leave the light on," Ken said, hopefully.

"There's no way you're going to get me to turn it off," I said.

Ken fished some peroxide out of our first-aid kit and poured it on the scratches. It stung a little but not much. I tied the mosquito netting across the front flap of the tent as best I could and turned the lamp so that it faced the entrance. It was going to be a long time till morning.

"I hope Mom isn't going to worry the whole time we're out here without her," Ken said.

"She knows we can take care of ourselves," I said.

When Mom had asked us if we wanted to help her in her studies of the Quechuan people we had jumped at the chance. We had stayed in Lima for two days getting ready, and then Mom had let us go up the Amazon while she had gone on to Bolivia. Mom had spent a long time studying the way different families around the world lived. We'd gone with her on many of the trips, but this was the first time we were expected to actually do observations ourselves.

I was glad that we would have Tarija Numa along. Tarija spoke English, Spanish, and the Quechuan language, and had lived as a child in the village we were staying in. She was the daughter of the woman who was working with Mom. She had flown with us from Lima, the capital of Peru, to Iquitos. But she stayed over in Iquitos to pick up some supplies while we took the long journey by motorboat up the Amazon to the small village. She was due to arrive in the morning, and I couldn't wait for the first streaks of daylight.

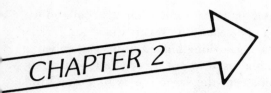

CHAPTER 2

"There are no bears in the Amazon," Tarija said, "at least not in this part of the Amazon."

"Then what do you think got Chris in the middle of the night?" Ken asked.

"I think it was two things," Tarija said. "One small thing, maybe a paca or something like that, and a bad dream. Pacas are like pigs with fur and no tail. There are some around here."

"And how do you explain the print on the sheet?" I asked.

"It could have been a paca," Tarija explained. "A little big, maybe."

"She's probably right," Ken said. "We have to get used to living in a jungle, I guess."

Tarija had invited us to eat on her uncle's boat and we started off. The jungle around us was really thick. Tarija went first. She carried a long-bladed knife she called a *cuchillito*, which she used to cut away the low-hanging vines. She was fourteen, the same age as Ken, and kind of pretty, thin, with brown hair and dark eyes. It was her people, the Indians who spoke the Quechuan language and were descendants of the Incas, that my mother was studying.

Ken and I had pitched our tent near the small Quechuan village. We were not allowed to stay in the village until we were formally introduced, Tarija said.

We got to the small, rickety pier where her uncle's boat was docked. He was short, fat, and mean-looking. He looked as if he didn't even know how to smile. Tarija spoke to him in Quechua and then came over to where Ken and I were watching a long string of ants walk along the edge of a path.

"What did you say this thing looked like last night?" she asked.

"I never really saw it," I said. "I thought it was pretty big, though."

"My uncle Inti says that the people are very afraid today," Tarija said. "They say they have seen signs of the *monstruo*. Strange smells, and strange noises at night. There is a legend that says that monsters move from place to place. Where the monsters go, you must leave."

Tarija went over and started talking to some of the Indians who were milling around near the edge of the water. They looked at her as she spoke, and then they turned quickly away from her and waved her away. She kept talking, but they wouldn't look at her. She came back over to Ken and me.

"They weren't happy with what you said?" I asked.

"They are good people," Tarija said. "But they have lived to themselves for many years. Now they are beginning to understand that there are other ways of living but they are not sure of what the other ways are. The old people want to move the village to some other place."

"They're afraid of the monsters?" I asked.

"Last week a young man was hurt," Tarija said. "Something hit him on the head in the darkness. There were scratches across his chest."

Ken and I exchanged glances. If something had attacked me and had scratched me, why was Tarija so sure it was a paca, and not the monster?

"What did you tell those people?" I asked.

"That I could make the monster go away," she said.

"And what did they say?" Ken asked.

"What my people always say," Tarija said, smiling, "that we will see."

"I don't believe in monsters," I said.

"Neither do I." Tarija shook her finger in front of her face. "I think that a paca is coming around and bothering people. Sometimes they smell very bad, too. Anyway, tonight we all sleep on my uncle's boat. He is working in Iquitos."

The boat was the same one that had brought us to Los Cauchos, almost a ten-hour trip up the murky Amazon River. I wasn't very happy with it. It was twenty feet long with a crooked little house built on it. There was an engine that had taken her uncle an hour to start before we pushed off and that he had to work on all the way up to Los Cauchos.

Tarija found some food, which was fish and fruit, and we sat on the boat and ate that.

"My father is dead," Tarija said.

"Sorry to hear that," I said.

"So where is your father?"

"Nobody knows," Ken said. "Our father was a mythologist. He studied people by looking at the things they believed in. One time he was flying to Mexico and his plane went down. We never heard from him again."

"He died?" Tarija leaned over and looked into Ken's face.

"No," Ken said. "At least I don't think so. But nobody knows what happened to him."

The fruit was sweeter than any I had eaten before and the fish was pretty good, too. It was kind of strange, though, sitting on a beat-up boat somewhere deep in the jungle having fruit and fish for breakfast.

Tarija said she had to go to talk to some people. She was trying to convince some of them to let their children go to Lima to go to school. They would stay with nuns, Tarija explained.

"Maybe I will help them with the village work, too," she said. "That way they will know that I am still Quechuan, and not a city girl."

"Can we help?" Ken asked.

"No." Tarija's face grew serious. "It's something I must do by myself."

We cleaned up after eating, and Tarija left to go into the village as Ken and I relaxed on the boat.

"It doesn't make sense," Ken said.

"That the Quechuas think that Tarija might have changed since going to school in Lima?"

"No," Ken said. "About the smell. According to Tarija the Indians said that the monster smells bad. They would know how a paca smells if they have lots of them around here."

Ken thinks really well, but he usually comes up with something I don't want to hear. And what I really didn't want to hear is that the Indians thought the monster smelled bad when it was one of the things I had noticed about the thing that had attacked me.

The day passed slowly. There was really nothing for us to do until Tarija arranged for us to be introduced to the people of the village.

She was gone most of the day. When she came back she said that we had been invited to eat with her people that evening. That was exciting news. Tarija asked us about what we did in school and Ken told her. Shortly before we were to go to dinner we had a visitor. Tarija smiled when she heard the loud "Hallooo" coming from the pier.

"Dr. Azeto!" Tarija said, standing. "How are you?"

"Fine!" The tall thin man put his hand on Tarija's shoulder. "And who are your friends?"

13

"Chris Arrow," I said. "And this is my brother, Ken."

"Oh, yes, your mother's Carla Arrow," he said. "I heard that you were somewhere in these parts. I hope you're enjoying yourself."

"So far," I said.

"I'm in and out of here all the time," Dr. Azeto said. "If there's anything I can do for you, just ask. As a matter of fact, I have the only radio communications to the outside world. So if you want to make a call I'm your man."

"Thanks," Ken said.

Dr. Azeto tipped his hat and started to leave, then turned back. "Oh, Tarija, Tomi said you were on the boat yesterday. Did you want something?"

"Just wanted to say hello," Tarija said.

"I see." Dr. Azeto nodded slowly. "Well, hello, and welcome back from your studies."

Tarija smiled as Dr. Azeto left the boat.

"He seems like a nice sort," Ken said.

"His boathand, Tomi, is croopy," Tarija said.

"Croopy?" I looked at her.

"You know, when somebody acts nasty all the time?"

"You mean *creepy*," Ken said.

"Creepy, that's the word. I went on the boat yesterday and he nearly chased me off."

"Just because you wanted to say hello to Dr. Azeto?" I asked.

"I was looking at some maps he had," Tarija said, frowning. "They were strange."

"Maps of what?" I asked.

"The village," she said, her frown changing quickly to

a smile, "and the shoreline. Maybe they're making a map of this area. I don't think there are any good maps. You have to know your way around. Come on, let's get something to eat."

We spent the day with Tarija looking around the village and being seen. Some of the children followed us around and I could tell that the older people were talking about us.

"You want to take a boat ride?" Tarija asked.

"Sure, do you have a boat?" Ken asked.

She didn't have one but she borrowed a small boat no larger than a canoe. Ken paddled while I sat as still as I could so the thing wouldn't tip over.

"The people use this kind of boat for fishing and for getting to places along the river," Tarija said.

The Amazon River was very wide where we were. The area around the pier had been cleared and you could just catch glimpses of the village through the trees. We moved easily through the water, going with the flow close to the shore. Once we had passed the pier area the trees and bushes were thick. We went for half an hour and then turned off the river into what looked like a stream.

"I hope you know your way around here," I said. The trees hung over the water's edge, their vines dipping into the dark brown water.

"This part I know a little," Tarija said. "The old people know every turn, every tree. It is wonderful."

"It sure sounds great," Ken said.

"But with more of the young people going to school and coming back to help our people that will be great,

15

too," Tarija said. "It's a lot of responsibility, you know."

Ken jumped as something slithered off the bank and into the water.

"What was that?" he asked, pulling the paddle from the water.

"Don't worry about it," Tarija said. "You only worry about things that bite you when you're in the jungle."

"I guess you're going to stay here," I said to Tarija. "Is that why you were saying it's a lot of responsibility?"

"I'll be back and forth between Lima, where the best schools are, and here in my village," Tarija said. "But that's not why I said what I did. It's a great responsibility because my people sometimes think that because I go to school I should never be wrong. They trust me too much."

"I think I understand," I said.

"We hear a lot of noises but I don't see very much," Ken said.

"Look!" Tarija pointed up.

There was a large bird, red and black with a tremendous beak, sitting in a tree just above us. It opened its mouth in a great screech and flew high in the sky, then swooped down in a large circle to another tree. It screeched again and was immediately answered from another tree. We turned, but couldn't see the other bird.

"There!" Tarija pointed to a tall tree that leaned to one side. There was a clump of branches with something on top of it that seemed to shine.

"There it is!" Tarija said. "That's the sun shining through its beak. Their beaks are very thin sometimes."

We continued along the small waterway that got smaller

and smaller as we went farther into the jungle. We turned the boat around and headed back for the Amazon.

"What happens if you take the wrong turn?" Ken asked.

"They find you after a while," Tarija said, grinning. "Maybe in two years, or three years."

Ken grinned, too, but I could tell he was glad when we got back to the Amazon.

It was hard work paddling against the flow of water. Other people passed us easily and Tarija said it was because they were used to paddling along these waters.

By the time we got back to the village both Ken and I were exhausted. Ken said he could use a shower.

"Come with me, then," Tarija said.

I didn't want to go, but she insisted. She took us along a small track away from the village. We walked a half hour before we got to a really dense part of the jungle with tall trees.

"Stay close," she said.

We did and it was hard work. In minutes we were dripping with sweat. In another minute it was raining.

"Your shower!" Tarija announced. "It always rains here."

It was clear that Tarija loved the warm rain in the forest. She held out her arms and let it run down her body. Ken wasn't as pleased and mumbled something about liking his showers to be in a bathroom.

"Don't be a crank," I said. "This is really great."

"If you think this is great you're all wet," Ken said. "Get it? All wet?"

I was too tired to moan.

We got back to the village and Tarija wanted to show us one more thing.

"I think we're too tired," I said. "Maybe tomorrow."

"It's worth seeing," she said. "And it will give you beautiful dreams."

"I'm too tired to dream," Ken said.

Tarija started pulling us and we went with her.

She was right. What she wanted us to see was the sunset on the Amazon. The sky was a murky gray except for the orange glow of the setting sun.

"Sometimes I used to sleep on the banks at night," Tarija said. "But you've got to be a little careful, because sometimes the crocodiles sleep here, too."

It had been a great day, but an exhausting one. I was glad we were sleeping on the boat. I wasn't sure about Ken, but I knew I was too tired to dream.

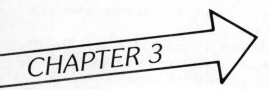

CHAPTER 3

It was barely dawn when I awoke with a start. There was a noise to my right and I looked to see Tarija putting on her sandals.

"Where are you headed?" I asked.

"Part of the legend of the monster," she said, wrapping the leather lacing of the sandal around her leg, "is that the monster can sometimes be bribed to go away. Last night some of the people put gifts in the clearing where they thought they saw the monster. I'm going to see if they are still there."

"Want Ken and me to come along?" I asked.

"Not yet," she said.

She moved around the cabin of the small boat gracefully and quickly. In a moment she was gone. It wasn't as if she just wanted to see if the gifts were gone. It was as if she were on some kind of mission.

Tarija had pointed out where her uncle kept food on the boat, and when Ken finally crawled out of his sleeping bag he tried convincing me that he could cook.

"I think you'd need a recipe to make tea," I said.

"You're so funny," Ken said. "I just have to remind myself to crack up!"

Ken got pretty mad about my kidding him and started sulking. He can do that very well and might have kept it up all morning if we hadn't heard all the noise outside. We looked out onto the nearby shore. People were shouting and pointing away from the village.

"Let's go take a look," I said.

When we got to the clearing we saw fruits, a pipe, and some cloth in a pile. They must have been the gifts, I thought. More important, right in the middle of them was the very still body of Tarija!

The Quechuan people were very upset. Two women went over and looked at Tarija. I went over too.

"Tarija!"

She moved, then lifted her head. I knelt by her side as she opened her eyes.

"Something hit me!" she said, rubbing the back of her head.

I looked to see if there was a bruise, but she looked okay. I helped her up and we started back to her uncle's boat. Some of the Quechuas spoke to her and she answered. They shook their heads and walked away.

Once on board the boat I asked her what had happened.

"I saw all the gifts the people had brought were still there," Tarija said. She picked up a piece of fruit and wiped it off on her leg. "I thought I saw a footprint on the ground behind the gifts and I went to take a look at it. I bent down and something hit me."

"Did you smell anything?" Ken asked.

"I don't remember," she said. "All I know is that I was hit pretty hard."

We talked about what would happen next. Tarija said that the next thing to do was to change the gifts.

"You mean maybe the monster didn't like those gifts?" Ken asked.

"Something like that," Tarija answered.

"And what happens if the monster doesn't take the next gift?" Ken asked.

"My people are an old people and there are many legends," Tarija said. "One legend is that if the monster does not want gifts it means that he wants a bride."

"A person?"

Tarija didn't look up at me but I knew that I was right. I had heard about people in remote areas making human sacrifices but I had never seen it before.

"That's pretty rough, isn't it?" I asked.

"The Quechuas are my people," Tarija said. "I have been to schools in Lima and there are many things I know that they do not know. But we are an old people and have many great things in our history. There are things about my people that even I do not understand. But I am learning."

"Here comes another boat," Ken said.

21

Tarija stuck her head out of the window and took a quick look.

"It's Dr. Azeto," Tarija said. "He brings in supplies twice, maybe three times a month. The government pays for part of them, and the people pay part."

The boat pulled alongside of us and Dr. Azeto leaned over the side.

"Hello, *chiquita,* have you seen the Arrows?"

"I ate them," Tarija called back.

"Are you looking for us?" I asked, popping my head out the window.

"You are to call your mother on my radio," Dr. Azeto said.

Ken and I went to the other boat. It was very clean looking and modern compared with Tarija's uncle's boat. On one side there was an ancient radio transmitter. The name COLLINS was printed on a shiny nameplate.

"I'll call for you," Dr. Azeto said.

We watched him as he tuned the transmitter, then made the call. After someone answered we waited a few minutes while they tried to hook up with Mom. It took a full five minutes of crackling and popping noises from the transmitter before Dr. Azeto handed me the microphone.

"Hello?"

"Chris?" It was Mom's voice.

"Hi, how's it going?" I said.

"Fine, and how are you guys?" she said. "Do you need anything?"

"We're okay," I said. "It's an interesting place."

"Is Tarija still translating for you?"

"Yes."

"I can't talk long." Mom's voice sounded as if she were in a tunnel. "Can I speak to Ken?"

I handed the phone over to my brother.

"Hi, Mom."

"Hello, how are you doing?"

"I'm having a monster of a time," Ken said.

"Do you guys need anything?"

"We could sure use some air conditioning," Ken said.

"I'm sure you could," Mom said. "I'm thinking that we could stay over in Lima for a week, just to relax when we're finished. You and Chris think about it, okay?"

"Sure."

Mom said good-bye and we thanked Dr. Azeto.

"He's not a real doctor," Tarija said as we got back into her uncle's boat. "He just calls himself that."

The Quechuas were having a meeting. Tarija said they were trying to decide what to give to the monster next. She said that she had to go see what they were going to do and that we could clean up the boat if we wanted to.

"Let's have a vote," Ken said, after she had left. "All those in favor of us cleaning up the boat say 'Aye.' "

"Any other ideas?" I asked.

"Were you wondering how Tarija got knocked out?" Ken asked.

"Yes," I said. "But I was also thinking that I didn't want to interfere with the customs of the Quechuas. I think that was what Tarija was saying."

"She said she saw a footprint," Ken said. "Maybe it's

still there. Checking that out wouldn't be much of an interference, would it?"

"We clean up a little first," I said. "We were the guests."

The clearing was deserted except for the gifts. We looked all around carefully. There were footprints but nothing unusual. We walked to the far edge of the clearing, where the bush was fairly heavy, and looked around there. I thought I smelled something, but I wasn't sure. Then, near a small puddle, I saw it. It was large, but not tremendous. I looked around and then knelt to get a better look.

"What is it?" Ken asked, coming near me.

"It's some kind of print," I said. "I don't know enough about tracking or animals to tell what kind."

"You want to follow it?"

"For a little way," I said.

We were doing a lot of looking around as we walked along following the footprints. I was in front and Ken was a little behind me.

"I think there are more than two feet," Ken said.

"You mean our monster has four feet?" I asked.

"Either that or two monsters," Ken answered.

I felt a cold chill go up my back as we went on. I was about to stop and say that maybe we should go back and get some help when I found that we were heading out of the dense part of the jungle. The footprints came out and down a small bank into a stream.

"You see footprints on the other side?" I asked.

"No, not from here," Ken said.

Ken wears glasses, but even with them he doesn't see

that well. I watched him go near the water.

"What are you doing?"

"Seeing if the water is shallow here," Ken said. "We can wade across."

I went to the edge of the water. The stream was only ten or fifteen feet across and I was sure that it was shallow. "I'll get a stick to see how deep it is," I said.

I broke off a piece of a branch as Ken took his shoes off. By the time I got back to where he had been he had started out into the water.

"Be careful," I said.

"It's not deep," he said. He was halfway across. "But it's mushy underfoot."

"Stay there a minute while I take a good look on the other side," I said. I didn't want him running into any surprises.

"It's harder to stand still than to walk," he said.

"There's a log in the water. Put your leg over that," I said.

Ken had just got one leg over the "log" when it suddenly moved! There was a splashing in the water and I saw Ken trying to get his balance. Then I saw what had done the splashing as a crocodile lifted its head! The water poured from its gaping mouth and shone like crystals on a wicked row of white, jagged teeth!

CHAPTER 4

"Ken! Run for it!"

I rushed to the water's edge and thrust the branch at the huge mouth. Ken had fallen and was trying desperately to get up! I brought the branch back and poked it again, as hard as I could. In the corner of my eye I saw Ken get to his feet. He took high steps toward the bank.

The crocodile was underwater. I could see his body twisting, sending up swirls of mud. He was coming straight toward me! I jabbed the branch directly at him just as his mouth opened. The force of his charge pushed me backwards. His mouth closed and he twisted in the water again. I tried to pull the branch back to ram it at him again when I realized that what I was holding was no more than two feet long. The crocodile had snapped the rest of it off!

"Chris! Get back on shore!"

I ran backwards as the crocodile disappeared from view. Ken was reaching for me and I grabbed his hand just as the crocodile's mouth opened again.

I jerked my leg away as the jaws snapped shut inches from me. I jumped for the shore and clawed my way up the embankment. When I reached the top of the small incline I turned back toward the water. There were circles where the water had been disturbed and splinters of wood from the branch.

My heart was pounding and my breath came in short gasps. I looked around for more signs of the crocodile.

"There he is!"

I jumped when Ken said that but he was pointing downstream about fifty yards. I looked to where he was pointing and then tapped him on the knee and pointed to a spot just below us where the crocodile I had just escaped from floated contentedly.

"You see the way he chewed that branch up?" Ken asked.

"Impressive, huh?"

"I guess so," Ken said. He started back toward the village and I followed as closely as I could without actually stepping on him.

"There is no such thing as this monster you talk about," Dr. Azeto was saying when we got to the boat.

"Then why did you tell the people it would be a good idea to move to another area?" Tarija asked.

"Because if it makes them happy to move then that is

27

what they should do," Dr. Azeto said. "The important thing is for the people of Los Cauchos to send their children to school so that they can move into modern times."

"Then what do you think hit Tarija?" Ken asked.

"Sometimes people imagine things," Dr. Azeto said. "The more you hear about monsters the more you think you see them. You hear that the monster smells so everything smells. If I told you that the monster marks his bride so that her spirit glows in the dark would you believe that?"

"Does he?" Ken asked.

"Of course not!" Dr. Azeto said. "That part of the legend is no more true than any of the rest. It is all nonsense!"

Dr. Azeto was about to leave. He asked us to help bring supplies from his boat and put them on the boat we were staying on, and we did. The Indian that he called Tomi was working with him. Tomi was a tall, powerful man who handled the big boxes of supplies easily. I got the feeling that Dr. Azeto was glad to leave, that he didn't particularly like the Quechuas or their myths.

"I even brought you clean washcloths," Dr. Azeto said. He tossed one to me, one to Ken, and one to Tarija.

"I bet that was Mom's idea," Ken said.

"I think you know your mother very well," was the smiling reply.

When Dr. Azeto left I remembered that he took the only radio with him. I couldn't contact Mom even if I wanted to.

"Did Chris tell you he was almost eaten by a crocodile?" Ken asked Tarija when Dr. Azeto's boat had left.

"You?" Tarija pointed a small brown finger at me.

"Ken was in the water first," I said. "When we saw the croc I held him off with a part of a branch. Only the croc bit right through the branch."

"You have to be careful when you go into the water," Tarija said. "If there is a crocodile in the water and he is big then he will eat you. If he is small he will try to eat you and that is almost as bad. That is why I carry my *cuchillito*."

Tarija patted the long knife she carried. It seemed like a good idea, but it hadn't helped her when she was in the clearing earlier.

Tarija told us to take some of the supplies and we started giving them out to the children. The parents seemed pleased but the children didn't seem too happy with the idea of pencils and notebooks. I think they would have preferred sweets.

Later another guy came to the camp. Tarija said that he was the government liaison man. His job was to help the people with their problems. It was his idea that the Indians show us how they used their blowguns.

"Some of them have shotguns now," Tarija said. "But even the ones with the shotguns can't afford bullets so they still use the blowguns."

The Quechuas tied a handkerchief around a small tree. Then they tucked a sheet of paper under one side of it. The paper had a black circle in the middle of it, and this is what they shot at.

Nine men shot at the black spot, which was about the size of the palm of my hand. They all stood twenty paces from the tree and shot in order. All nine men hit the paper but only two hit the black spot, and Tarija gave each of them a piece of cloth as a reward.

"Will you ask one of them if I could try the blowgun?" Ken asked.

Tarija asked and one of the men produced a shorter blowgun for Ken. He gave him a straw pouch of darts, showed him how to put a piece of cotton on the end to fit the barrel of the blowgun, and then let him blow sharply into the carved mouthpiece. Ken couldn't reach the tree with his arrow and they all laughed.

I was getting tired of eating fish every day even though Tarija told me it was better than most of the Quechuan food.

"Maybe they catch fish and maybe they don't." She said it matter-of-factly. "When they don't they eat yams and corn, or maybe *sit'ikira.*"

"What's that last thing?" Ken asked.

Tarija tossed Ken a piece of a plant that looked like cactus. He tried it and said that it tasted like a mouthful of juicy string.

We got to bed early that night and I spent some time thinking about taking pictures in the morning.

I must have been asleep for a minute when I felt something shaking me. I jumped up quickly. It was only Ken.

"What's the matter?"

"Something's wrong with Tarija," he said. I could tell

by how wide his eyes were that he was nervous about
something.

"What?" I asked.

"She's glowing in the dark!"

CHAPTER 5

"How do you know she's growing?" I asked.

"Not growing," Ken said, pushing his glasses back up on his nose. "She's *glowing*. And I know because I saw her. I heard somebody moving around in the boat and it was her."

I got up slowly and sniffed the air to see if I smelled the same thing I had on our first night in the Amazon. I didn't. I couldn't imagine Tarija glowing. What I thought was that somebody else might have been on the boat. I slipped into my pants and tennis shoes. Then I went to the small pantry that Tarija slept in. I thought about going around the outside of the boat and looking through the window, but changed my mind. I knocked on the door.

"*Qué?*" Tarija's voice sounded sleepy.

"It's Chris," I said. "Can I see you for a minute?"

There was silence for a moment and then the door opened. I jumped back nearly a foot. Tarija *was* glowing!

"You have a mirror around?" Ken asked. He was standing behind me.

"You wake me up to ask for a mirror?" Tarija asked.

"I think you'd better take a good look at your face," I said. "Your hands, too."

Tarija looked down at her hands. Her palms were glowing a dull blue. She rushed past me quickly to a closet and brought out a tin mirror.

"I-eee!"

She dropped the mirror and started looking around the cabin. Ken found a light on the box we used for a table and handed it to her. She turned on the light. When she did she wasn't glowing.

"I'm marked by the monster!" Tarija looked in the mirror again.

I wanted to tell her to calm down. I wasn't sure why because I didn't feel particularly calm, but it seemed the right thing to say. But before I could speak she had run out into the night.

"I don't," I said to Ken as firmly as I could, "believe in monsters."

"Neither do I," Ken said. "You want to sleep in the same sleeping bag tonight?"

We went out to look for Tarija and found her on the shore. It was easy to find her. All we had to do was follow the glow. We ran to her and reached her just as she fell to the ground.

"Tarija! Are you all right?" Ken reached her first.

"Carry me back to the boat," she said, her voice nearly a whisper.

"Maybe we shouldn't move you," I said.

"Carry me back!" she whispered hoarsely.

I took her in my arms and started back toward the boat. Ken went ahead. Tarija didn't weigh much but my knees were shaking badly by the time I bent over to get into the low doorway.

"Close the curtains on the boat," Tarija said.

"Are you . . . are you okay?" Ken held the lamp near Tarija's face.

"I'm okay," she said. She sat up.

"Tarija, I don't know what's going on," I said. "But I think we can use some help. Maybe we can get Dr. Azeto to call the police at Iquitos."

"No," she said. "I don't know what is going on, either. But I know there are no monsters."

"Then who . . ." Ken pointed toward her hands. "You know."

"I don't know," Tarija said. "But somebody is trying to make me believe there are monsters around. I don't believe it!"

"They're trying to make me believe it, too," I said. "I guess I don't believe it. I mean, if you don't."

"I think there's a reason," Tarija said, "but I can't think of what it is. And why me?"

"Can I ask you a personal question?" Ken asked. He had his head turned to one side, the way he did when he had an idea. "Do your people like you?"

Tarija shrugged. "They used to love me," she said. "The government pays most of the money to send me to school in Lima, but the people of the village pay the rest. That is why I love them so. They think I am very smart."

"That probably explains it, then," Ken said. He looked satisfied with himself.

"Explains *what?*" I asked.

"Well, if you wanted to convince everybody there was a monster around," Ken said, "the easiest way would be to convince the smartest person, and then everybody else would believe it, too."

"Wait a minute, he's got something there," I said. "Were you in a sleeping bag tonight?"

"No, it's too hot," Tarija said.

"Then somebody could have come in and put something on your hands and face to make you glow in the dark."

"And my people know about you," Tarija said. "They know that you are the sons of a famous person. So if we are scared, then they might become scared."

"That's only a theory, though," I said. "What's not a theory is that you were knocked out yesterday, and that other strange things have been happening. I think we should call the police."

"No, there's got to be a reason that people are being frightened," Tarija said. "If we call the police we won't know the reason. Also, there is another problem."

"What's that?" I asked, not really needing another problem.

"I went to school in Lima. My father went to school

35

in Lima and he is from this village. If we bring the police to this village people will think that is what going to school does. It brings people to the village who don't belong here to ask questions and to look around. No, we must find out what is going on. I can speak to the chief, who will do what I ask him for a while."

"And after that?"

"My people are very good at defending themselves!" Tarija said.

"That would do the same thing," Ken said. "That would bring the police here, too."

"We'll make a trap," Tarija said. "Maybe we can catch a monster!"

"With what?" Ken asked. "What can you catch a monster with?"

"If the monster is trying to scare me," Tarija looked from me to Ken, "then I will be the trap!"

I didn't like the idea. Tarija was Ken's age. She seemed older than that but I knew she wasn't. "Did you see anything when you went outside?" I asked.

"No. But someone is watching us!" she said. Her face tightened as she spoke. "That is why I had you carry me back inside, to show how afraid I was."

"Well," I said, "we can't risk having you hurt. We have to get help."

"Then my people don't mean anything to you," Tarija said. "You are just afraid for yourselves."

"Look, why don't you go into the village tonight," I said. "Let me think about it."

We walked Tarija to the village. She went to the small

grass-and-bamboo house of a friend. It was built on sticks, nearly six feet above the ground, to keep it dry during the rainy season. Tapiza was an ancient woman with thousands of little wrinkles crisscrossing her face. She wore a man's hat and a short, dark jacket. We talked with her awhile before we left. Then we went back to the boat.

"How come," Ken was saying as we went slowly back toward the boat, "Tapiza was saying that all the people in the village were wearing special necklaces to keep the monsters away if they don't believe in monsters?"

"You believe that going under a ladder gives you bad luck?" I asked.

"Of course not," Ken answered.

"If you saw a ladder up ahead would you go under it?" I asked.

"Of course not," Ken said, again. "But everybody knows I'm chicken."

Ken and I talked most of the night. I thought he was scared. I knew I was scared. We finally drifted off, still dressed, as the sky was getting light.

When I woke there was the sound of birds outside the boat and the warmth of the early sun against my skin. Ken was still asleep and I decided to let him stay that way.

In the light of the new day things didn't seem nearly as scary. I thought we would probably figure out a logical explanation to the whole thing. I was just thinking that Mom would have really laughed if she knew we were worried about monsters, when I heard a loud thump outside the cabin. I told myself not to be so jumpy, but I still went to take a look. What I saw was a flaming arrow stuck into the deck.

"Ken! Wake up!" I called to him and he jumped immediately.

"What's up?" he asked, scrambling to his feet.

"We've got trouble!" I looked on the pier to see who might have shot the arrow, but there was nobody there.

Ken came to the window, saw the arrow, and started backing away. "Let's get out of here," he said.

"No, wait," I said, starting for the door. "I'll throw it overboard."

"No!" he shouted. "It's next to a can of fuel!"

I started to ask him if he was sure when the fuel exploded, slamming me into the wall. In a moment the boat was burning. We ran to the door. It was locked!

CHAPTER 6

The fire spread quickly along the deck. I tried banging on the door but it didn't budge. I turned to see Ken and saw him sitting calmly on a folding chair.

"What are you doing?" I asked.

"Waiting for you to get the door open," he said. "You will get it open, won't you?"

I was hoping that I would. The windows were too small for me to get out of them. I figured Ken would fit through one of them if I knocked out the side panels. I found a large wrench and smashed at it. It splintered under the blow but most of it remained in place. I hit it again and again, knocking out pieces of the frame. Finally, I had enough out for Ken to squeeze through.

"Ken, get through here!"

He came to the window as the back of the boat started to lift in the water. We were just beginning to sink. I pushed him through the window as quickly as I could.

"Hurry!"

I waited a minute as he got to his feet and then made for the door. The flames from the fire were higher now and I could see the inside of the wall beginning to buckle. I heard Ken fumbling with the lock as the back wall of the cabin began to buckle.

"Hurry!"

The boat groaned and the front end went deeper into the water. Then the door opened and I rushed through.

We had drifted away from the pier and I yelled to Ken to swim for it.

"There are man-eating piranhas in the water!" he yelled back.

"You're not a man yet, so jump!"

I'm on the swimming team in my school and it was a short swim so I figured I'd be okay. I let Ken jump in first. Maybe it was thinking about the piranhas, but he got to the pier in nothing flat. He climbed up the side and I was a step behind him.

"You okay?" I asked.

He was out of breath but he was okay. He fished through his pockets, found his glasses, and turned to me. There was a piece of a plant caught on the side of his glasses. "There was rope around the cabin-door lock," Ken said.

"Just what we needed," I answered.

"Can we save the boat?" he asked.

I turned and looked for the boat. It was drifting down-river, burning as it went, like a Viking burial boat. I watched as it slowly sank, then disappeared. A thin wisp of smoke came up from where it had been.

"Look who's coming," Ken said.

I looked. It was Tarija and some of the other Quechuas.

"What happened?" she asked when she reached us.

"Nothing much," Ken said. "Somebody just locked us in the cabin and tried to burn us to death."

He stood and walked away from her.

Tarija dropped her head. I'm not sure if she understood everything that Ken had said, but I know she understood how he said it. He had almost been killed and he was pretty sure that Tarija either had something to do with it or knew something about it, and I wasn't sure if he was wrong.

The liaison man had come to Los Cauchos in a boat, and I figured we could grab a ride with him.

"You want to see about heading out of here?" I asked. "It's pretty clear that somebody wants us gone."

"Not us," Ken said. "There's no reason to get rid of us."

"Then who?"

"I don't know," Ken said. "Maybe one of the Quechuas, maybe even Mom."

"Mom?"

"Maybe they think if we're here we're going to bring more people and find out something about this place."

"What's there to find out?" I asked. "We're in the Amazon jungle, a full day away from anything anybody would want. The Indians don't have anything that I can see."

"Me, either," Ken said. "But there's got to be something going on."

"You think you were a little rough on Tarija?"

"I guess so," Ken said.

We spent the afternoon putting our tent back up again. I was glad that we hadn't brought it to the boat. Usually if we went someplace we would leave a lot of the equipment behind because it was cheaper than taking it back home. We had thought about giving the tent away but now we had to sleep in it.

We were just putting the finishing touches on it when there was a loud commotion from the village. Ken went outside and looked.

"That guy Tomi is over there saying something," Ken said.

We left the tent and went over to where the noise was coming from. Sure enough, Tomi was standing in the middle of a group of Quechuas.

We stood to one side of the people milling about him and just watched. He was holding something next to his head, as if it had been hurt.

"Do you want to know what he is saying to the people?" Tarija startled me.

"Do you want to tell us?" I asked.

She looked at me and screwed her mouth up. "He says

that somebody tried to set fire to his boat this morning. He wants to know if they trust you."

"You believe that?" I asked.

"No," she said, "but I don't know if I can trust you either. Are you going for *la policía?*"

I looked at Ken. "No," I said. "I don't think we want to do that."

"Then help me." Tarija put one hand on my chest and the other on Ken's. "Until this is over we will have one heart."

"One heart," I said.

"One heart," Ken repeated.

"One thing," I asked. "Is there anything that we should know about this village?"

"No," Tarija answered. "Years ago there was a rubber company here and some of the people used to work for it. When the rubber company left they gave the land to my people. Most of the land around here doesn't belong to anyone, not legally, anyway. This land belongs to my people, which is why they want to keep it."

"Are there still rubber trees around here?" Ken asked.

"Yes, but not enough to make money," Tarija said. "That is why the company left."

"That probably explains the strange sounds I heard the other night," Ken said.

"What strange sounds?" Tarija asked.

"Didn't you hear the weird music?"

"No," I said. "And what explains it?"

"That bit about the rubber trees," Ken said. "The strange

music was probably made by a rubber band! Rubber band! Get it?"

"Ken, shut up!"

Tarija went back to the village. She said there were things she had to do. I told her to be careful, but I knew she wouldn't be.

Ken and I decided to kill two birds with one stone. I think it was because we were a little afraid of staying in the tent after our first night.

"I saw a cowboy movie and this worked just fine," Ken said.

We had rolled up blankets and clothes and put them in pants and shirts to make dummies of ourselves. We found melons that we hoped would pass for heads in the darkness of the tent in case anyone looked in. Ken even put an extra set of glasses he had with him on his dummy.

We sat up waiting for it to grow dark. Then we sneaked out of the tent. We knew that a goat had been taken to the clearing as a second gift to the monster. We had seen the people of the village take the animal.

We looked around the tent and started in the direction of the clearing. I went first and told Ken to keep his hand on my shoulder. We went as fast as we could without making a lot of noise. It still took us a pretty long time.

When we got to the clearing we knelt down behind a large tree. We could see the goat dimly. It was standing in the middle of the clearing, tied to a stake that someone had driven into the ground.

"You think there are any snakes around here?" Ken whispered in my ear.

"I hope not!" I whispered back.

It was incredibly hot and I could feel the sweat running under my shirt. I shifted position, trying to get comfortable.

"Baa-aaa."

The goat lifted its head and bleated at the sky. Ken tightened his grip on my shoulder.

I thought I heard a rustling noise and listened carefully. Nothing.

"Ken," I whispered as softly as I could.

"Wh-what?"

"You hear anything?"

"No."

"Baa-aaa."

The goat was pawing at the ground. It tried to jerk away from the stake it was tied to.

"Baa-aaa."

"I don't think anything's coming tonight," Ken said. "You want to leave?"

The smell hit me like a slap in the face! I put my hand over my nose. The goat was bleating! Then there was another sound. It was a growl that changed into a roar as something crashed through the bushes on the other side of the clearing. I couldn't see what it was except for the fact that it was huge! It bent lower as it neared the goat and lifted it off the ground with one hand or paw or whatever it had. Then it lifted itself to its full height and growled again! It was moving away from the goat in long lumbering steps and headed right for Ken and me!

CHAPTER 7

The thing, whatever it was, stopped for a moment. I was trying to decide what to do when Ken made up his mind and took off.

I started off after Ken. The moment I started I thought I heard a growl behind me. I figured Ken to be headed for the tent and I ran in that direction, stumbling over branches in the darkness. I fell heavily, knocking the wind out of myself for a moment. I heard the thing behind me, still headed in my direction and still growling.

Then, a few yards ahead of me, I saw a light.

"Chris!"

I scrambled to the light and Ken. There was a big tree, its trunk thicker than an oil drum, and Ken was crouched next to it. I didn't know why he had stopped running and thought he might be hurt. I knelt down next to him and he turned out the light.

"You hurt?" I asked.

"No."

I put my arm around him and we listened carefully. We heard the growling and what sounded like leaves rustling as the thing moved through the darkness. Then, suddenly, it stopped. The silence was eerie. It was as if even the jungle itself were afraid to make a noise.

Patches of sky could be seen through the thick branches. Where the sky was clear I could see stars. The only sound I heard was Ken's breathing in my ear. His leg was against mine and I could feel his body shaking.

The odor still filled the air. It seemed to be getting stronger and I wondered if the thing was getting closer.

Then I heard a twig snap off to my left. Ken's head jerked in that direction and I knew he had heard it, too. I didn't see anything for a while, and then I did. At first it was just a shadow moving slowly past the branches. Then, as it passed a small clearing, I saw what looked like a gigantic animal, but no animal that I had ever seen before!

It stood upright, like a human, but was taller than a human could ever be. Its ears were pointed like a wolf's but the face of the thing was flat. It turned in our direction and my blood ran cold! The quick, black eyes darted back and forth, the mouth was a red gash filled with fierce rows of jagged teeth!

I felt Ken tense but I wasn't sure which of us was shaking more.

The monster, after looking around, moved on in the

same direction he was headed. After a while we couldn't see him through the thick bush. Now and again he would stop and growl or some small animal would scurry from his path, and we would have an idea of where he was.

"Let's get out of here!" I spoke into Ken's ear. I started out slowly through the underbrush, keeping as low as I could.

"Chris! I can't move!"

I went back to him quickly. "What is it? Your legs?"

"No, I just can't move!"

"Come on, you're just scared," I said, hoping that I was right. "You can move. I *know* you can."

I looked at his face. He nodded to me, but I could see, even in the dim light, that he was just hanging on. Slowly, almost painfully, he got up and we started making our way back to the village.

We went back to the tent. Nothing was disturbed. But there was no way we were going to spend the night there. Instead we went to the middle of the village and sat near a large flat rock the Quechuas used for grinding corn. That way we figured that we could see anything headed for us.

We sat on the edge of the stone, close together, until we drifted off to sleep.

"Chris!"

It was Tarija who woke us. I saw Ken just stretching a few feet from me. It was morning and the sun was already high above the tall trees that surrounded the village.

"How long have you been here?" she asked.

"I don't know for sure," I answered. "Most of the night, I guess."

"The monster didn't take the goat," Tarija said.

"What does that mean?" Ken had joined us. He was running his fingers through his hair to get it in place.

"That he wants a bride," Tarija said. "I was the one marked. Some of the people think that I should be tied to the stake because that is the only way to make the monster happy."

"No way," I said. "That's ridiculous."

"You said you would help us." Tarija looked me in the eye. "If I am willing to be tied to the stake, you should be willing to watch for the monster."

"You said your people were good at defending themselves." Ken had his glasses off and was squinting at Tarija. "You could get a few of them, with their blowguns, and they could protect you."

"Whoever is revolved in this knows a lot about Quechuan legends," Tarija said.

"You mean *involved*," I said. "You figure a Quechua is doing this, but why?"

"That's what we have to find out, *muchacho*," Tarija said.

"We saw it last night. We went to the clearing to see if it took the goat."

"What did it look like?" Tarija asked. "No—no, don't tell me!"

She shuddered.

"You said that some of the people want you to be tied to the stake," Ken said. "What do the others want?"

"They think that those were the old ways that we have to leave behind. They know the old ways were not so good."

"What do they want to do?" Ken asked.

"The way the legend goes," Tarija said, "is that once the earth was ruled by giants and monsters and other strange creatures. Each was so terrible that none of the others dared to go near it. The storms are the echoes of their battles.

"To stop such battles the god of gods gave each creature the land that was his father's, which they can never leave. Once a monster is angry he will remain angry until he gets what he wants. But he cannot leave the village of his father."

"The monster's father?" I asked.

Tarija nodded.

"So some of the people think they should leave and settle someplace else?" Ken asked. He was standing and I could see he had an idea.

"Yes," Tarija said.

"What happens if you just leave?" Ken asked.

"I would not leave my people," Tarija said.

I watched my brother pace for a few seconds and then begin rubbing his nose with the palm of his hand.

"I have an idea," Ken said. "I don't like it very much but it might work."

"What is it?" I asked.

"If Tarija can find a boat, we can all start toward Iquitos," Ken said.

"I told you that I would not leave my people," Tarija

51

said. "We who have some education have to find a way to serve our people."

"But you said that you don't believe in the monsters," Ken said. "But something, or someone, is trying to scare you into leaving. If you left by yourself, just took off in a boat with me and Chris, what would happen?"

"They would be glad because I am gone," Tarija said. "Or maybe not glad, because they want me to convince the other people in the village to go."

"Right." Ken was pleased with himself.

"What are you two talking about?" I asked.

"About finding out who wants Tarija away from here," Ken said.

Tarija did find a boat. It wasn't more than a rowboat with an outboard, but it ran.

"The man I borrowed it from said that it was a lucky boat," Tarija said.

"Did he say that it won't sink?" Ken asked, looking at the boat suspiciously.

"It will be all right," Tarija said.

Ken looked worried once we started out toward Iquitos. The small motor *putt-putt*ed noisily as the boat glided along the mighty Amazon River. We weren't making a lot of headway but the trip was pleasant.

"How far is it to Iquitos?" I asked Tarija.

"In this boat we'll be traveling all day and half the night," she answered.

We waved to some small boys swimming in the water near the shore. I thought about the crocodile we had seen and asked Tarija why the boys weren't afraid.

"The boys are too hard to catch," Tarija said. "They look for fish."

I wondered if I looked fishy.

It began to rain lightly. The rain never lasted long in the dry season and it wasn't very heavy, either. I pulled a slicker over me and lay back in the boat. Between the steady noise from the boat's engine and the heat I was almost asleep when I heard Ken give a loud clap.

I looked up at him and saw this great look on his face as if he had just been elected the first fourteen-year-old king of the world. He pointed behind us.

I turned and saw two boats headed toward us. They were Indians, and I guessed that they were Quechuas. In the first one a barrel of a man with a chest full of white hair stood with something in his hands.

"Those are the old ones," Tarija said.

"The ones who believe in the monster?" Ken asked.

"Yes," was the quick answer.

The boats were catching up with us pretty quickly and I got to my knees just as the barrel-chested guy threw something. It was a rope with a rock attached to each end. I got one arm up as it reached me, but the rocks still spun around my body and slammed into the small of my back! In a moment I felt myself being jerked into the water.

I heard Tarija screaming and turned to see both her and Ken go flying into the muddy Amazon. We were being attacked!

CHAPTER 8

Underwater, I tried to free myself from the rope. I kicked until I got to the surface and took a deep gulp of air. I was at the side of the boats. I went back under and tried to twist out of the rope. I couldn't tell if I was twisting the right way or not. Then I felt a pull. I was being hauled to the surface. In a moment I was out of the water again. I felt hands on me and knew the Indians were pulling me into the boat.

I didn't resist. I saw that they were trying to pull Ken into the other boat. He was kicking and fighting all the way. Finally, one of the Indians had to jump in and grab him. I watched them wrestle him into the boat.

Tarija was the last. They pulled her into the boat with

me and she came without a struggle. Tarija had been right. All of the Indians that were in the boats were older. The boats turned and we were headed back to Los Cauchos.

I tried asking a few questions on the way back but I didn't get any answers. The Quechuas didn't speak at all, to me or to Tarija. As we reached the pier I saw someone watching from the shore. It was Dr. Azeto's helper, Tomi! He watched for a few minutes as the boats were landed, and then disappeared among a crowd that had gathered at the shore. We were helped off the boat, and a moment later I stood on the pier waiting for them to take me someplace but they didn't. Several of them stopped and spoke to Tarija but they just walked past me and went about their business.

"Ken was right," Tarija said. "The people who took us from the boats are those who believe in the monsters. They said they don't wish me harm, but it is the good of the village they must consider."

"What happens next?" I asked, as Ken walked up to us.

"I have to wait until the chief decides what to do," Tarija said. "He is going to have a meeting with the village leaders this evening. I don't think they will decide anything without talking to me. They have great faith in me. Still, I'm a little afraid."

Tarija put one of her hands on my shoulder and the other on Ken's. She looked at us for a long moment, smiled, and then turned and went into the middle of the village. I saw her sit next to an old woman. A moment later, they were grinding corn.

Walter Dean Myers

"I've got a feeling that this whole thing has to do with Tarija's going to school in Lima," I said. "The chief has put his faith in her because she's going to school, and because she represents a new way of living for the village. If someone makes her look bad they can probably convince the chief that education isn't so hot after all."

"Could be," Ken said. He had taken off his shoes and was wringing out his socks. "There's too much going on, though. You got monsters running around, you got things sneaking into our tent, you have somebody telling some of the Quechuas that they should bring Tarija back when it looks like she's leaving. There has to be something else that *somebody* wants."

"Maybe somebody just wants to take over the chief's job," I said. "The chief looks pretty old."

"Could be," Ken said. He didn't look as if he believed it, though.

"If not some young guy looking to be chief, then who?"

"I bet if we could find out who talked those guys into bringing Tarija back we would know something." Ken had put his shoes back on and was lacing them up.

"I saw Tomi, the guy who works for Dr. Azeto, waiting for the boats when we came back," I said. "You think he has something to do with it?"

"What's he doing here?" Ken asked. "I thought that Dr. Azeto had left."

"So did I, but I'm sure that I saw Tomi."

"You want to find him and talk to him?" Ken asked.

"Nope. But let's do it anyway."

We started looking around for Tomi and didn't see him.

I caught a glimpse of Tarija as we went through the village. She was with several older women who were putting flowers in her hair. They seemed happy enough.

We didn't see Tomi in the village, but we did see Dr. Azeto.

"Hello, *amigos*," he said. He was drawing a picture and some small children were gathered around him, watching. "How are you today?"

"Fine," I said. "I thought you only came here once a month?"

"Sometimes if I am called on the radio I come more often," he said. "But since the radio is not working I thought I would check on things before I headed back to Iquitos."

"I think they're getting ready for a party here or something," Ken said.

"Yes, I guess so." Dr. Azeto made a graceful line on the drawing pad before him. "But I don't have the time to concern myself with such things. As soon as Tomi sees if there is anything they need we'll be on our way again."

"Any chance of getting a ride to Iquitos?" Ken asked.

"I'm afraid not," Dr. Azeto said. "Sometimes we have to make emergency stops. They could be anywhere along the Amazon River and last as long as a week. I couldn't guarantee when you would reach Iquitos."

"I understand," I said.

"Let's get back to the tent and get some rest," Ken said.

We both had the same idea. If Tomi was checking what supplies were needed and Dr. Azeto was on shore, it would be a perfect time to check out his boat.

We took the long way to the pier. Ken stayed on the shore as a lookout and I went along the pier. I stopped across from the boat and looked around. No one from shore seemed to be paying me any attention. In a moment I was aboard.

I got below deck as quickly as I could. The first thing I heard was the crackle of the radio. Someone was speaking in Spanish. I picked up the mike and tried speaking into it. The answer came back in Spanish. I tried speaking in English again, the answer came back in Spanish again, and I gave up.

I heard a whistle. I looked through the window and saw Ken walking quickly along the shore. Then he stopped and started talking to someone. It was Tomi!

I started to swing up the stairs to the deck when something caught my eye. It was a picture, something like the one that Dr. Azeto was drawing in the village. I recognized a group of trees that were in the center of the village, but not the large structure behind them. It was a pretty fancy building. There was even a name on it, Posada de los Cauchos.

I got to the deck in two jumps. I could see Ken still talking to Tomi. I hopped up on the pier and tried to look casual as I walked away from the boat.

I told Ken about Dr. Azeto's radio working and about the picture. He asked me if I could remember exactly how the words were spelled. I said yes and we went to find Tarija to translate them for us. It was easy to find her, but we couldn't get near.

There was a group of women around her. She was dressed

in a long robe. Young girls were putting necklaces on her and some kind of red powder on her face. Suddenly I realized what the party was all about. They were preparing Tarija to be the bride of the monster!

CHAPTER 9

I went over to the crowd to see what I could find out, but I couldn't understand what they were saying. Dr. Azeto had one arm around Tarija and was shaking his head. When Tarija saw me and Ken she quickly turned away from us.

"Ken," I whispered to my brother. "Let's get out of here."

"What's going on?" he asked.

"They're getting ready to give her to the monster as a bride," I said. "Remember when she said it was time to do what came next?"

"This is it?"

"This is it," I said. "And we'll be there again tonight."

"You think we might be too scared to even go near

the clearing?" Ken asked, looking at me hopefully.

"I think we'll be scared," I said. "But if Tarija is brave enough to offer herself for her people, then I think we have to be as brave."

The plan sounded better in my head than it did when I told it. I looked at Ken and I knew that he didn't think a lot of it, especially the part where we would sneak back into the jungle after dark.

The first time we had waited near the clearing to see if there really was a monster, it had been warm. This time it was steamy hot. The jungle felt like a great big oven. The plan was simple. We were to hide in the bushes. Ken was going to hide on one side of the clearing and I was going to be on the other. We would wait to see if a monster came. If it did I was going to stand up, wave a light, and then run like crazy!

I remembered how slowly the monster had run the first time. I also remembered that it had left the clearing fairly quickly after it knew we had seen it. Ken would free Tarija and the two of them would follow the monster at a safe distance to see where it went. If we found where the monster was coming from, I thought, maybe we could get help and trap it.

Tarija was taken to the clearing just after sunset. Ken and I waited until well after that before we started off, Ken from one direction and me from another, through the jungle toward the clearing.

I found the clearing easily, keeping as low as I could. I could see Tarija sitting by the stake where the goat had been tied. She looked a lot more relaxed than I would have been.

We waited.

Hours went by and nothing happened. My shirt was soaked with sweat and the mosquitoes were having me for lunch and dinner. I didn't hear anything from Ken on the other side of the clearing. I figured that the monster, whatever it was, knew that something was up and was staying away.

I was nearly exhausted when, suddenly, the smell came. I had been sitting in some tall grass with my back against a tree. The first thing I did was to look behind me. I didn't see anything.

I heard the screeching of a bird and, a moment later, an answering screech. The second one seemed to come from near the clearing.

Then there was the loud half growl, half bark that I knew was the monster! Tarija, who had been lying on the ground near the stake, lifted herself up. I could see that her hands were tied behind her back. She got to her knees and looked around. I ducked down.

The monster roared again and I felt my stomach turn to jelly. Then I heard something crashing through the jungle near me. I flattened myself on the ground.

Had it seen me? Was it coming after me?

I put the palms of my hands on the ground, ready to push myself up as quickly as possible to fight back. I imagined the monster jumping on me as I lay there.

I opened my mouth wide and tried to keep the sound

of my breathing low. I heard the thing go by me and breathed a sigh of relief. I lifted my head as much as I dared. Tarija was on one knee. I saw that not only were her hands tied behind her back but one leg was tied to the stake. She couldn't escape!

There was another roar from the monster, the loudest one yet. But this time it was followed by a scream! Then I saw it. It was gigantic! It crashed out of the trees from the side of the clearing. I ducked again and this time, when I lifted my head, I saw the monster lift Tarija high above its head!

CHAPTER 10

I got to my feet and raced across the clearing! I couldn't
let the monster take Tarija. I just couldn't!

Ken was screaming! He had panicked. The monster
turned just as I was about to tackle it. Its cruel face stared
down at mine and for a moment I thought it was laughing
at me. I must have stopped for a second, frozen on the
spot. I saw the monster's arm move and reacted a split
second too late. The force of the blow sent me reeling
backwards and down to the ground. I tried shaking my
head. I looked around, only half understanding what I was
seeing as images spun crazily before me. The last thing I
saw before passing out was the monster crashing through
the bushes with Tarija!

I awoke hours later in the house of Tapiza. Dr. Azeto

was putting cold water on my forehead. I opened my eyes and tried to figure out where I was.

"Ah, my brave friend." Dr. Azeto smoothed my hair back. "I see you are back with us."

My mouth was too dry to speak and I nodded. Ken came over to me and looked at me. He was looking in my face to see if I was all right and I tried to smile.

"Do you want something to drink?" Dr. Azeto asked.

I nodded again and he gave me a gourd of what tasted like fruit juice.

"I have to go back to the boat," he said. "I'll try to go downriver until I find a radio to report this incident to the police in Iquitos. Your brother and Tapiza will take good care of you, I'm sure."

Tapiza, the old woman, smiled as Dr. Azeto said something to her in Quechua and patted me on the shoulder.

"How do you feel?" Ken asked.

"Terrible," I said. "What happened?"

"Nothing after that thing knocked you out," Ken said. "Chris, I wanted to help you but I was afraid."

"Hey, that's okay," I said. "I sure didn't do myself or Tarija much good. Did . . ."

"Yeah." Ken looked down. "He took her with him."

Tapiza gave me some soup. I drank it and soon I was feeling better. Ken told me that Dr. Azeto was leaving in the morning for Iquitos, and that he said we should go with him.

I hadn't had a lot of sleep the night before and I was still pretty tired. I drifted back off to sleep and woke up hours later. It was already afternoon. Ken was lying on a mat with his eyes open. I got myself up and went over to him. He turned away as I got near but not before I could see that he had been crying.

"Feeling bad?" I asked.

"Yes," he said. "When that thing came into the clearing I was too scared to move. When he grabbed Tarija I just tried to get away."

"Don't feel bad," I said. "Maybe if I had spent a little more time thinking instead of jumping up and attacking the monster I might have come up with something."

Ken still had his face to the wall. He looked miserable. I knew he would never forgive himself if we found out that something really bad had happened to Tarija. He liked her a lot.

"Chris?"

"Yes?"

"What are you going to tell Mom?"

I thought for a long moment. Nothing that I thought about sounded good. "I'm going to tell her that the monster took Tarija and that, after he did, we decided to get her back."

Ken sat up. "How are we going to do that?"

"I don't know," I said. "Why don't you see if you can come up with something."

Thinking was what Ken did best. Sometimes it was a pain, but there were times when his thinking really pulled us out of a tight spot. I hoped this would be one of those times.

We left Tapiza's house and went out into the village. People were gathered in the middle of the village. They were in a large circle. The men were on the outside and the women and children on the inside.

"They've been like that since we got back to the village," Ken said. "When they saw Dr. Azeto carrying you and he told them that the monster had taken Tarija, they got pretty scared. They're going to another place to start a new village."

"You know when they're leaving?"

"At night," Ken said. "They don't want the monster to see them going. Dr. Azeto said we could stay on his boat tonight and leave with him in the morning."

"Then we've got to do something before tonight," I said. "We've got to find where the monster took Tarija."

"I think I know," Ken said. "I mean, I think I know where it seems he took her, but it doesn't make any sense."

"Where?"

"If nobody saw the monster in the village then he had to take her into the jungle," Ken said.

"That's obvious," I said.

"But it didn't come from the jungle."

"How do you know that?"

"Remember the first time we saw it? We were waiting near the clearing and we saw it coming from the far side. The *same* side it came from when it took Tarija."

"But there's not much on that side," I said. "There's about fifty yards of jungle and then the river."

"Right," Ken said. "And there's another thing. When it left with Tarija it left in the same direction it came from."

"You want to take a walk by the river?" I asked.

Walter Dean Myers

"Sure," Ken said, nodding.

We went back to our tent and I changed into my tennis shoes. Ken took the small blowgun he had got from the Indians, and we set off. I could tell he was scared, and I knew that the blowgun wouldn't do much good if we ran into the monster again, but I didn't say anything to him.

We started at the clearing and went slowly through the thick stand of tall trees. Every swaying limb made my heart beat faster. Every bird flying low or animal scurrying in front of us made us hold our breath, afraid that it might be the monster.

We got to the river without seeing anything. There were a few prints along the edge, but I couldn't make anything of them. I remembered the crocodile we had run into before. It wasn't a pleasant memory.

We walked up and down the riverbank for a long while without seeing anything interesting. Then we sat down and tried to think of something else to do.

"What's that?" Ken asked.

"What?"

"Over there."

He was pointing out over the water. I looked and didn't see anything. Then I saw some bubbles on the water. I shielded my eyes from the sun and watched them awhile.

"Some kind of animal?" I asked.

"Could be," Ken answered. "But I saw them a little while ago, and now I see them again."

"What do you think?"

"A super mammal kind of thing, maybe," Ken said.

"Like a monster?"

"Like a monster," he said. "Or a machine."

I was one of the best swimmers on our high school team, especially underwater. But that was in a pool, and without crocodiles or poisonous snakes or whatever else they had in the Amazon. Still, I knew I couldn't live with myself if I didn't at least take a look.

"It's a long shot," I said, taking off my shoes.

Ken didn't answer.

The bubbles were coming up about ten feet from the shoreline. I raced through the possibilities of what they could mean. I started out with the monster, which wasn't exactly reassuring. Then I thought about a crocodile, but there were too many bubbles for a crocodile. I told myself to stop thinking. I was just getting myself scared.

"Chris, be careful," Ken said as I stepped into the water.

I figured there was a shelf and I edged toward it slowly. The water got deep some six feet away from the shore, which really surprised me, but then I remembered what Tarija had said about the water being deep enough for boats to dock.

Under the water was as murky as above and I spent a few seconds just getting my eyes accustomed to it. When I had I looked around and saw the bubbles coming straight up from beneath a shelf. I looked around, but didn't see anything that looked as if it was going to get me. Then I came up again, waved to Ken on the shore, took a deep breath, and made my dive.

The water was deep. I stayed near the shelf, moving myself along with my hands on what looked like steel rods planted in the ground. When I reached the shelf I ran

69

into something I never expected. There was a tube coming from under the shelf, and the bubbles were coming from it. I followed the tube and saw that it led to some kind of light. I swam a little farther and found what looked like a narrow tunnel. I wasn't sure how far it went up or how easy it would be to get back down. I moved up slowly, trying to figure out when I would be halfway out of breath. I'd need enough oxygen to get back out.

I was nearly out of breath when I neared the top, but I pushed up a little farther. My lungs began to burn and I knew I had either to turn back at once or go ahead and hope I found some kind of air pocket. I had just decided to go back when the water cleared and I saw I was only a foot from the top. I gave myself one more push and came up into an underground cave!

The cave was lit by lamps connected to a generator. There were chairs and a table as well, as if somebody lived in the cave. And there, tied to one of the chairs, was Tarija!

"Chris!"

I was still tired from the swim up the hole and took an easy stroke toward her. Then she called out again.

"Behind you!"

I turned around in the water and saw something on the other side of the cave. It was the monster!

CHAPTER 11

I gulped in as much air as I could and headed for the hole leading out from the cave. When I heard the splash I didn't have to look to see what had jumped into the water. I knew it was the smelly, hairy beast that had carried off Tarija! At first I had trouble finding the hole, but I saw the tube and followed it. I found the opening and pulled myself through it as quickly as I could.

The sides of the cave seemed to narrow as I went through, and I could feel the rock cut my shoulders. I came out swimming for my life! The monster was right behind me. I saw it swimming toward me with short, powerful strokes! I turned away and pulled for the surface. I didn't know how good a swimmer it was, and I didn't want to find out!

I got to the water's surface and started heading for shore. The water was almost shallow enough to stand in but I wasn't sure of the bottom so I decided to swim.

Behind me the monster broke into the open as well. It started swimming toward me. It was gaining on me with every stroke. Then I felt a sharp pain in my shoulder. It was as if someone had stuck a knife into me. I grabbed at my shoulder and felt something slippery moving in my hand. It was a piranha, the deadliest fish known to man!

My shoulder was bleeding and I knew piranhas were driven crazy by the smell of blood. If there were enough of them they could strip a person's bones clean in minutes. My only hope was that there weren't enough of them around to get me before I got out of the water.

I struggled to my feet. I was only yards from shore. I jerked another of the deadly fish from my arm as I stumbled forward. They were ripping at my pants! I could feel a thousand little cuts as I rushed the last few yards and flung myself on the shore. I turned and saw them swimming in furious circles just yards away from me! There were more coming every second! I pulled my feet away from the water's edge.

Confused and bleeding, I stumbled along the river's edge toward where I saw Ken waving. I looked back into the water. I saw the monster swimming downstream, away from the piranhas. It was trying to work itself away from the fish and toward the shore before the fish spotted it. I grabbed a stone and threw it at the monster. I didn't know why, or what good it would do, but I heaved it.

Ken was still shouting something but I couldn't pay

him any attention as I tried to stop the blood from my arm. The pain was unbelievable.

I looked up to see the monster standing. The fish were getting near it, and it was running toward the shore. It didn't seem very much like a monster anymore. I realized it was coming in pretty close to Ken, and I waved to my brother to come toward me. He was pointing behind me. I turned and nearly fainted at what I saw. There were two more monsters!

I stopped in my tracks and then started to run up the incline toward the jungle. It was too late. One of them cut me off and grabbed me in a headlock! I punched out as best I could but it didn't seem to be bothered. Then I felt something trying to lift my legs. If they threw me back into the water the piranhas would finish me for sure! If they dragged me into the jungle I wouldn't be much better off. I struggled and kicked for all I was worth. I broke free for a wild moment and tried to run again. They caught me and I felt myself being dragged toward the river.

One of them screamed! It was a loud, blood-curdling scream and it made me fight that much harder! I twisted and turned and kicked even more. Then I was free. I was being held by only one of the monsters now and I tried a judo hold. Nothing! He had me around the neck and was choking me. Then, all of a sudden, he let me go! I fell to the ground and rolled away from where I thought the river was. I looked up and saw the monster going toward the jungle.

I twisted around to see where the other one was but he

wasn't in sight, either. The only thing I saw was Ken running toward me.

"C'mon!" he shouted.

He started running along the river toward the village. I took a few steps and fell.

"Ken!" I called out to him. "I can't make it!"

"You've got to make it, Chris!" He turned around. "You've *got* to make it. Our lives depend on it!"

I pulled myself to my feet again and went after him. Every step was agony. Every breath made my whole chest hurt. We got to the village and Ken ran toward the pier.

I followed and watched him stop just as we reached Dr. Azeto's boat.

"We've got to get the boat," Ken said, "or I think we're through!"

"Let's look for Dr. Azeto!" I said.

"No!" Ken looked at me wild-eyed. "We've got to take the boat ourselves!"

I didn't know what my baby brother was up to, but I hoped he had something going. He motioned for me to stay on the pier as he jumped onto the boat. A moment later he came flying off with Tomi racing after him. The stocky Indian had murder in his eye and a wicked-looking knife in his hand. I ran toward Ken, hoping he would remember something we had done months ago in a gym class in school.

He slowed down just enough for the guy chasing him to almost touch him. Then he jumped as I dove for his feet. He went over me and I hit the ankles of the guy behind him. The guy went down with a crash and rolled

74

off the pier into the water. I was on the pier, the breath knocked out of me. I looked up and Ken was untying the boat. A moment later he had got it started and I was on my knees trying to collect my thoughts. I couldn't believe it as Ken started pulling the boat away from the pier. Was he leaving me?

"Jump!" he shouted. "They're coming!"

I looked and saw one of the monsters heading my way. The guy that we had ditched into the river was climbing over the edge of the pier. I got myself up somehow and ran along the pier. I threw myself over the water and just managed to make the boat. Ken turned it around and headed away from the pier.

"We've got to get out of here!" Ken yelled.

"We've got to go back and get Tarija!" I said. "She's under the water in a cave!"

"Can you get her out?"

"Probably not," I called out. "But I can try!"

Ken guided the boat back to where we had first seen the bubbles.

"You mean she's under there?" Ken asked.

"Yes!" I shouted over the roar of the engine. "And what are we going to do about our friends while I'm under the water?"

"Did you see where the bubbles came from?"

"A tube," I said. "But that's not the problem—"

"How wide is the opening?"

"Narrow. I could just squeeze through."

"Then there's got to be another way out," Ken said.

"What are you going to do while I look for it?"

"I'll think of something!" he said.

We had reached the place where we had seen the bubbles and I looked for them. I also looked for piranhas. I didn't see any and hoped I wouldn't. Just in case, I took Ken's shirt. It didn't fit too well but it covered up the spot where I was hurt, and I hoped it would keep the smell of the blood down awhile.

I jumped into the water. I could hardly move, I was so scared. I looked for the tube, found it, and moved quickly along the shelf. A big flat fish saw me, bumped me with his nose, and moved on.

I found the opening and wiggled up, expecting to feel the piranhas biting me at any moment.

Tarija was still tied where I first saw her. I swam over to her and pulled myself from the water. The water in the cave had risen. It was past Tarija's ankles. I untied her quickly.

"Ken thinks there's another way out of here," I said.

"There!" She pointed toward a large rock. "Behind there!"

I rushed to the rock with Tarija a half step behind me. Just as I started to push it I heard voices on the other side!

CHAPTER 12

Even if Tarija hadn't been tied up for hours and I hadn't been running around like crazy, I didn't think we could handle anything. Especially if it came monster-sized!

I looked around quickly and saw the wire that went to the light. I grabbed it and gave it a pull. Nothing. Tarija grabbed it with me and together we pulled as hard as we could. There was a noise like cats fighting and then we were plunged into total darkness.

We flattened ourselves against the wall. In the darkness I could hear Tarija's breathing. There were some grunts and the rock moved away from the opening. Whoever or whatever it was outside must have seen that the lights were out. Nothing happened for a long time and then, slowly, something started into the cave.

There was some light that came in from the outside and I could see what looked like a long brown leg. There were feathers around where the knee should have been! I held my breath and tried to get behind the rock so I wouldn't be seen.

The shadowy figure slipped by me and I could hear it fumble in the darkness. It made a noise that I thought could have been a word in another language, and Tarija squeezed my shoulder.

The owner of the other voice came in and the two of them started talking. Their voices were low, but one of them sounded familiar.

I knew one thing, that if they got the lights back on we were in for it. I took Tarija's hand off my shoulder and patted it gently. I was hoping that she would know that I meant for her to stay still for a while.

I listened carefully to see if I heard any other noises from outside. Nothing.

The lights came on for a split second, and then only dimly. When they did I saw two men near the end of the wire that Tarija and I had pulled out. Any minute they would get it together! Then they would see us and . . .

I reached for Tarija again so I would know exactly where she was. Then I put both hands on the rock. It wasn't a moment too soon. The lights came on! I looked down and saw Dr. Azeto and his man staring up at us! They were both dressed as monsters from the neck down, and their monster heads were next to them on the ground.

I pulled down on the rock as hard as I could and sent it crashing toward the two half-monsters!

"Let's get out of here!" I grabbed Tarija's hand and dove for the opening that the rock had covered. I ran into a thick underbrush but fought my way through it. As soon as I got out I turned and pulled Tarija with everything I had. She got one leg out but someone had her other leg. She bent over and bit the hand around her ankle. There was a cry of pain and the hand released her ankle.

For a wild moment I thought about looking for rocks to throw down into the hole but instead I followed my first instinct. I ran! I started toward the river, looking for Ken, but Tarija dragged me down and pulled me toward the village.

"We've got to get to the river!" I said. "Ken's waiting there with Dr. Azeto's boat!"

"No!" she said. She rushed ahead of me and I followed as quickly as I could. I figured once I got to Los Cauchos I could find the river and my brother easily enough.

When we ran into the center of the village the Quechuas were just beginning to leave. They stopped when they saw Tarija. She rushed past a group of children, pulling me with her, up to a group of old men.

I stood trying to catch my breath and looking back toward the river as Tarija spoke to the Indians in their own language. One of the men pointed at me and Tarija said something to him.

"What did you say to them?" I asked. I saw an old man speak to some younger ones, who ran toward the river.

"I told them everything that happened," Tarija said. "He asked me where your brother was and I told him. He has sent warriors to put things right."

There was a lot going on, but I saw that all the men had their blowguns and other weapons. The Quechuas were the descendants of the Incas, and now they looked like it.

The wait seemed forever. The entire village seethed with excitement. Women took their children to the center of the village to a large house. Some of the men seemed to be just standing around, but I soon saw that they had surrounded the village.

"Don't be afraid," Tarija said. "These men have not forgotten their bravery, and they are not stupid. It is the people who work against us who have forgotten our history."

"I'm not worried," I said, holding my breath.

Tarija patted my hand and then pointed to the far end of the village. There were two groups of men coming into the village. One group of Quechuas was leading Dr. Azeto and his men. I recognized Tomi. They had taken off the top of the monster outfit that he was wearing. Now he looked ridiculous. Several of the others had parts of the outfits that they had made out of what appeared to be old animal skins and feathers. They looked a lot less fierce with their hands tied behind their backs and their heads down.

Dr. Azeto was talking as quickly as possible, waving his hands and touching his chest as he tried to explain how innocent he was. No one was listening to him.

The other group was escorting Ken. He looked pretty happy with himself. Tarija pointed toward him and laughed.

They brought Ken to where we stood and one of the women put his arms around me. I put my arms around my brother and hugged him for a long moment. Then we both put our arms around Tarija. Our adventure in the Amazon had ended.

"So the Quechuas never did believe in the monsters?" Mom said. "I wouldn't think they would. Not most of them, anyway."

We were in our hotel room in Lima, going over our adventure with Mom. Ken was eating fruit and Tarija was sitting cross-legged on the bed.

"I guess some of them weren't that sure, though," I said. "They had all heard the legends and everything. Then, when Dr. Azeto bribed a few of them to pretend they were scared, the ones who weren't too sure looked to see what the chief and Tarija were going to do."

"The chief, he said to me, 'What is your advice, Tarija? You have gone to school!' " Tarija snatched a banana that Ken had just peeled.

"And what did you say?" Mom asked.

"I said, 'I don't know,' " Tarija said. "And the chief said that it was good advice. He said it was very wise to know when you do not know something."

"That's when they decided to find out by letting things go on," I said.

"And they were depending on Tarija to know when things were getting out of hand," Ken said. "When Dr. Azeto's men brought Tarija and us back, the chief and the leaders knew that the answer to the mystery was right in the village, but they couldn't figure out who was responsible. Everyone trusted Dr. Azeto."

"He always spoke about education and about how wonderful it was that people from our village could go to school and even to Lima for more education," Tarija said. But when he found out that the government was going to build a hospital near our village everything changed."

"That," I said, "I don't see."

"That I understand," Mom said. "Dr. Azeto knew that a hospital is often the center of a larger community. Often entire cities are built around a good health-care center. He also knew that the rubber company had built the pier years ago. Even though it doesn't look that good the dock was built deep enough for large boats. Remember, there aren't many places along the Amazon that are suitable for large boats."

"So, if my people were afraid to stay in the village he could buy the land from them cheaply," Tarija said. "And he could have a ferry service right to the front door of the lodge he planned."

"Posada de los Cauchos," I said, remembering the drawing I had seen on the boat.

"And the map that Tarija saw was a surveyor's map," Mom added.

There was a knock on the door. It was Tarija's mother. She was an attractive woman not much taller than her daughter. Ken and Tarija went over the entire story again for her sake and she made a big deal over how brave Ken had been.

"And how did you know they weren't really monsters?" Tarija's mother asked.

"The power of positive panic," Ken said. "When I saw Chris coming up out of the water and those two 'monsters' chasing him I didn't know what to do. I just panicked and shot at them with the blowgun."

"But there wasn't any poison on your darts," I said.

"I knew that," Ken said. "But they didn't. They panicked more than I did. That's when I figured there had to be men under all that fur."

"You are really very smart," Tarija's mother said.

"And there was one other thing," Ken said.

"What was that?" Mom asked.

"The piranhas," Ken said. "As soon as I saw them I knew something was fishy. Get it? Fishy?"

Tarija, her mother, Mom, and I all groaned at the same time. The real Ken Arrow was back.

ABOUT THE AUTHOR

Walter Dean Myers has written many novels for young adults, including two ALA Notable Books, *Fast Sam, Cool Clyde, and Stuff* and *It Ain't All for Nothin'*, and two ALA Best Books for Young Adults, *The Young Landlords* and *The Legend of Tarik*. Mr. Myers lives in New Jersey.